First Edition 10 9 8 7 6 5 4 3 2 1
ISBN 978-1-4847-0643-5
F383-2370-2-14311
Library of Congress Control Number: 2014946559

Printed in China

Visit www.disneybooks.com

Sofia the First

A Royal Mouse in the House

Written by Bill Scollon
Illustrated by Grace Lee

Disney PRESS
Los Angeles • New York

The day of the Pet Talent Show has finally arrived! Students from Royal Prep line up on the palace grounds to sign in.

"Wait until you see Clover's dance," Sofia tells Amber.

"Yes," answers Amber. "But my peacock, Praline, is so pretty she'll easily win first place."

Outside the castle, the princes and princesses groom their pets and work on their tricks.

Zandar tosses a ball to his elephant.

"Look, Mom!"

Freedo is holding James up in the air by his feet. "James! Be careful," says Queen Miranda.

"Attention, everyone, the Pet Talent Show will soon begin."

Suddenly, Princess Hildegard rushes in, late as usual, holding her pet mink, Lulu. "Wait," she calls.

"Please fill out this form, noting your pet's special talent," Baileywick says.

"Lulu does gymnastics, like somersaults," Hildy says. "But because she's so small, she gets really nervous around crowds. . . . Whoops!"

"Oh, no! Lulu, come back!" cries Hildy as she chases after her pet.

whoops!

"We should help Hildegard," Sofia tells Clover. "You look in the castle, and I'll look for them outside."

Meanwhile, Hildegard runs through the
castle searching for her pet mink.

Hildy pauses before an old, ornate mirror.
"Oh, I'm a mess!" Hildy says, patting her
hair back into place. "I wish I could
understand why Lulu ran away. I
would totally win this competition
if I were—"

At that very moment,
a mouse scurries past.

A mouse!

Suddenly, Princess Hildegard turns into a mouse! "Oh, no!" Hildegard squeaks when she sees her reflection. "This can't be! I'm so small and everything is so big! Help!" she screams in a tiny voice.

Just then, Clover hops down the hall. His big ears pick up the faint sound of someone crying.

It's a mouse!

Clover asks the mouse what's wrong.

"Clover, it's me, Princess Hildegard," the mouse says.

Clover can't believe it. "What happened?" he asks.

"I don't know," Hildy answers. "What should I do?"

"Sofia will know," says Clover. "Hop on!"

Squeak

Squeak

They find Sofia in the courtyard looking for Lulu.

"Hildy, is it really you?" asks Sofia.

"Sofia. It's me, Hildegard. I don't know what happened. I was just looking for Lulu, and suddenly I became a mouse!" replies Hildy-mouse.

"Do you think someone cast a spell on you?" says Sofia. "We need Cedric's help!"

Sofia leads Hildy and Clover to Cedric's workshop.
"I know the perfect counterspell," Cedric says.
He holds his wand up high, mumbles a few magic
words, and POOF!

Eek!

But the spell doesn't work. Hildy is still a mouse.
Except now she is blue.
Hildy-mouse is so embarrassed that she runs away.

Hildy-mouse runs out of the castle
into the courtyard filled with kids and pets.
"Look!" cries Amber. "A mouse!"
Hildy-mouse is scared. Everyone is so big compared to her.

Hildy races across the courtyard
and scampers through an open door
into the castle, where she feels safe.

But Hildy ends up in the kitchen,
where the cook scares her even more.
*Small creatures are nothing but
helpless,* thinks Hildy, looking around
for the quickest escape.

She spots a mousehole and runs
inside.

Shoo!
Shoo!

At last Hildy feels safe.

Then she turns to see a family of mice behind her giving her a funny look.

"I am not a mouse!" cries Hildy. "I am a princess."

Just as Hildy-mouse steps outside the mousehole and sees Sofia and Clover, Lulu finds them.

"Oh, Lulu, thank goodness you're back! Now I know being small is no fun when everyone is bigger than you," says Hildy-mouse.

"Hildy, what happened right before you became a mouse?" asks Sofia.

"I was in the hallway," Hildy recalls. "A mouse ran past me and I screamed. Then I turned into a mouse."

Clover speaks up. "Can you show us *where* it happened?"

"Certainly," replies Hildy-mouse.

"It was in this spot," says Hildy-mouse.
"The Magic Mirror!" gasps Sofia.
"Hildy, you were standing right in front of it."
"That's what turned me into a mouse?" asks Hildy.
"Make a wish and we'll find out," says Sofia.
"Magic Mirror, turn me back into a princess again!"
says Hildy.

With a *POOF!* a swirling cloud covers Hildy-mouse
and leaves Princess Hildegard in her place!
"Oh, thank goodness, I'm back," says Hildegard.
"I thought I would be a blue mouse for good!"

Outside the castle, Baileywick is waiting. "Princess Hildegard, where have you been?" he asks. "I'm sorry. The talent sign-ups are closed."

"Does that mean we can't be in the show?" Hildegard asks sadly.

"I'm afraid so," says Baileywick. "It wouldn't be fair to the others."

"Okay, let's go home, Lulu," Hildy says.

"Wait," says Sofia. "They can take our spot."

"Are you sure, Princess Sofia?" asks Baileywick. Sofia and Clover nod. "We're sure," she says.

"Lulu," says Hildy. "We'll do this together. You'll be great!"

"Good luck!" Sofia tells Hildy.

Lulu leaps high and passes through a hoop. The audience applauds wildly.

After the talent show, Baileywick announces the winners. "First place goes to . . .

Princess Hildegard and Lulu!"

Sofia and Clover can't be happier.
Neither can Hildegard and Lulu, who now know that even when you're small, you can do great things!

The End